The Tree of Life

An Amazonian Folk Tale

written by Charlotte Guillain ☼ illustrated by Steve Dorado

 Raintree

Raintree is an imprint of Capstone Global Library Limited, a company incorporated in England and Wales having its registered office at 7 Pilgrim Street, London, EC4V 6LB – Registered company number: 6695582

www.raintree.co.uk
myorders@raintree.co.uk

Text © Capstone Global Library Limited 2015
The moral rights of the proprietor have been asserted.

Edited by Daniel Nunn, Rebecca Rissman, Sian Smith, and Gina Kammer
Designed by Joanna Hinton-Malivoire and Peggie Carley
Original illustrations © Capstone Global Library Ltd 2014
Illustrated by Steve Dorado
Production by Victoria Fitzgerald
Originated by Capstone Global Library Ltd
Printed and bound in China by RR Donnelley Asia

ISBN 978 1 406 28132 3 (paperback)
18 17 16 15 14
10 9 8 7 6 5 4 3 2 1

ISBN 978 1 406 28139 2 (big book)
18 17 16 15 14
10 9 8 7 6 5 4 3 2 1

British Library Cataloguing in Publication Data
A full catalogue record for this book is available from the British Library.

Characters

Coati, a villager

Coati's brother,
Saki

Other villagers

Long, long ago in a village in the rainforest, there was not much food for people to eat. People lived on roots and berries, but no fruits had ever grown on the trees.

One day, a young man called
Coati was feeling very
hungry. He wandered deep
into the forest to look for
food. Suddenly, he noticed a
delicious smell and began
to follow it.

The smell led Coati to a clearing, where an amazing tree was standing.

The tree was covered in many types of colourful fruits. Coati ate the delicious fruits until he was full.

Coati went back to his village, but he did not tell anyone about the tree. Every day, he went back to the tree and ate the fruit in secret.

Coati's brother, Saki, watched him disappear into the forest every day. Saki wanted to know what Coati's secret was.

So one day Saki followed Coati.

When Coati saw Saki had followed him, he was shocked. But he shared the fruits with his brother. Saki said they must tell the rest of the village about the wonderful tree so everyone could eat well.

Coati was not happy, but the brothers went back to the village and told the other people about the tree. The next day they brought the villagers to the tree, and everyone ate and ate. They cut down all the fruits on the branches.

Coati became worried when he saw how much fruit they were cutting down. He tried to make the villagers stop, but they were too busy eating to listen.

Suddenly, a child was stung by a wasp. The villagers blamed the tree and cut it down.

The tree crashed to the ground, and silence fell as water started to gush out of the tree stump. The water kept flowing until the forest began to flood.

The people ran to the
top of a mountain.

When the floodwater went down, the people returned to their village. Now the forest was full of trees, each with a different fruit growing on its branches. The people could eat well, but from that day they always respected the forest and shared the plants that grew there.

The end

The moral of the story

Many traditional stories have a moral. This is a lesson you can learn from the story. The moral of this story is not immediately clear. Maybe Coati should have shared the fruit with the other people from the start. Or perhaps the moral is that we need to take care of the plants in the natural world. If we are too greedy, we might destroy the things we need to survive. What do you think?

☸ ☸ ☸

The origins of *The Tree of Life*

Nobody knows who first told the story of *The Tree of Life*, but the story comes from the Amazon region in South America. People used to tell stories like this for entertainment before we had television, radio, or computers. The story has been passed on by Amazonian storytellers over hundreds of years, with different storytellers making their own changes to it over time. Eventually, people began to write the story down, and so it has spread around the world.